GRANDPARENTS' HOUSES

Poems about grandparents
selected by Corrine Streich

Pictures by
Lillian Hoban

GREENWILLOW BOOKS / NEW YORK

To my children's grandparents —C.S.

For P.H., B.H., E.H., and J.H., with love —L.H.

ACKNOWLEDGMENTS

Permission to reprint copyrighted poems is gratefully acknowledged to the following:

Margaret Walker Alexander, for "Lineage" from *Jubilee* by Margaret Walker, Yale University Press, 1942.

Associated University Presses, for "The Passing Years" by Reuben Elsland from *The Golden Peacock, an Anthology of Yiddish Poetry*, edited by Joseph Leftwich, published by Robert Anscombe & Co., Ltd., London 1939, reissued 1944.

William Bedford, for "The Kitchen" from *Strictly Private*, edited by Roger McGough (Penguin 1981).

Doubleday & Company, Inc., for "Deep in the Mountains" by Saibara, translated by Hiroaki Sato from *From the Country of Eight Islands*, edited and translated by Hiroaki Sato and Burton Watson, Copyright © 1981 by Hiroaki Sato and Burton Watson.

Gerald Dumas, for excerpts from "Afternoon in Waterloo Park."

Robert Friend, for "From My Mother's House" from *Leah Goldberg: Selected Poems*, translated by Robert Friend, Menard/Panjandrum, 1976.

George Allen & Unwin (Publishers) Ltd. (British rights), for "Blessings on Gentle Folk" from *The Book of Songs*, Arthur Waley, translator.

Grove Press, Inc., for "Blessings on Gentle Folk" #164 from *The Book of Songs*, Arthur Waley, translator, Copyright under the Berne Convention.

William J. Harris, for "A Grandfather Poem," Copyright by William J. Harris.

Hill and Wang, a division of Farrar, Straus & Giroux, Inc., for "Grandparents' Houses" from *Good Morning, Last Poems* by Mark Van Doren, Copyright © 1972, 1973 by the Estate of Mark Van Doren.

International Literature and Arts Program, directed by Bonnie R. Crown (British rights), for "Deep in the Mountains" by Saibara, from *From the Country of Eight Islands, An Anthology of Japanese Poetry*, edited and translated by Hiroaki Sato and Burton Watson, Anchor Books/Doubleday 1981.

Persea Books, Inc., for "Return of the Village Lad" by Alfred Lichtenstein from *German Poetry 1910-1975: An Anthology in German and English*, Michael Hamburger, editor and translator, Copyright © 1976, 1977 by Michael Hamburger.

Leroy V. Quintana, for "The Legacy II."

Anthony Sheil Associates Ltd., for "Gifts from My Grandmother" by E. M. Almedingen from *Tomorrow Will Come*, published by John Lane, The Bodley Head, Ltd.

Greenwillow Books, a division of William Morrow & Company, Inc., 105 Madison Ave., N.Y., N.Y. 10016. Printed in U.S.A. First Edition
10 9 8 7 6 5 4 3 2 1

Library of Congress Cataloging in Publication Data Main entry under title: Grandparents' houses. Summary: Fifteen poems about grandfathers and grandmothers by poets from China, Japan, the United States, and other countries.
1. Grandparents—Juvenile poetry.
2. Children's poetry.
[1. Grandparents—Poetry.
2. Poetry—Collections]
I. Streich, Corrine.
II. Hoban, Lillian, ill.
PN6110.G83G73 1984
808.81'3520432   84-1604
ISBN 0-688-03894-8
ISBN 0-688-03895-6 (lib. bdg.)

They must have magnets in them, set
For certain persons only; set
For those that came—hear the high
Voices—suddenly in summer
Up the leafy road, exclaiming
Who knows what till they arrive
In silence at the door—surprise,
Surprise—then in, familiarly,
As if they now were where the pull
Of dark invisible iron had brought them:
Children once removed, magic
Offspring with the eyes of others
Most at home here of all places.

GRANDPARENTS' HOUSES / by MARK VAN DOREN

My grandfather
How have you been passing the days?
Happily, as old as I am
I could be grandfather to anyone
for we
have many children

ZUNI GRANDFATHER

Deep in the mountains, are you cutting trees, grandpa?
Are you carving trees, are you carving those trees,
carving trees, grandpa?

Translated from the Japanese by Hiroaki Sato

DEEP IN THE MOUNTAINS / by SAIBARA

Grandfather never went to school
spoke only a few words of English,
a quiet man; when he talked
talked about simple things

planting corn or about the weather
sometimes about herding sheep as a child.
One day pointed to the four directions
taught me their names
    El Norte
Poniente   Oriente
    El Sud

He spoke their names as if they were
one of only a handful of things
a man needed to know

Now I look back
only two generations removed
realize I am nothing but a poor fool
who went to college

trying to find my way back
to the center of the world
where grandfather stood
that day.

THE LEGACY II / by LEROY V. QUINTANA

I look at this picture of that old man,
My grandfather,
And my eye drops past the full-blooming beard
To his hand, pale, strong, as hairless as the
Top of his head; a hand used to pens and desks,
Used to pipes, pump handles, hoes, a horse's flank;
A hand knowing of heavy Bible, wafer pages,
Golden edge and gothic script; an 1860 hand
That knew the 1860 things. And it startles me
To think that my shy hand once lay in his,
As his lay in his grandfather's who flourished
While Napoleon, to name one, still lived.
From me to 1800—
And one pale hand the link.
A touching chain, and longer than we think.

from AFTERNOON IN WATERLOO PARK / by GERALD DUMAS

A grandfather poem
Must use words of great dignity.
It cannot
contain words like:
Ubangi
rolling pin
popsicle
but words like:
Supreme Court
graceful
wise.

A GRANDFATHER POEM / by WILLIAM J. HARRIS

The locusts' wings say 'throng, throng';
   Well may your sons and grandsons
Be a host innumerable.

The locusts' wings say 'bind, bind';
Well may your sons and grandsons
Continue in an endless line.

The locusts' wings say 'join, join';
Well may your sons and grandsons
Be forever as one.

Translated from the Chinese by Arthur Waley

from BLESSINGS ON GENTLE FOLK

GRANDFATHER   I wish I were already old
               I would get myself a heavy staff,
               And buy a snuff-box too, maybe,
               And sit on my front-step and laugh
               Seeing people rush by hurriedly,
               As if they had no time to stay,
               Hurry, hurry all the day.
               Or maybe
               I would just go
               Through the streets calm and slow,
               With a smooth face,
               Marvelling at the unruffled pace
               With which over the stones
               I move my old bones,
               Step by step,
               Step by step.

                         Translated from the Yiddish

THE PASSING YEARS / by REUBEN ELSLAND

Grandmother of mine
how have you been passing the days?
Happily, our child
surely I could be grandmother
to anyone
for we
have the whole village as our children

ZUNI GRANDMOTHER

My grandmothers were strong,
They followed plows and bent to toil.
They moved through fields sowing seed.
They touched earth and grain grew.
They were full of sturdiness and singing.

My grandmothers are full of memories—
Smelling of soap and onions and wet clay
With veins rolling roughly over quick hands
They have many clean words to say.
My grandmothers were strong.
Why am I not as they?

LINEAGE / by MARGARET WALKER

Grandmother, you gave me the wealth of detail. You taught me to love grass and moss, ants and butterflies ...You gave me my first trees and my first sunset, mushroom hunts and the bliss of long walks.

GIFTS FROM MY GRANDMOTHER / by E. M. ALMEDINGEN

S crubbed like a cube of sunlight,
  The kitchen walls and the kitchen floor
Whitened throughout my childhood,
Spreading like an October morning.

Wild with blackberries and streams.
At the sink, grandmother laundered.
At the table, grandmother read and sewed,
Dissecting the new neighbors.

On the doorstep she dreamed of trees.
And the kitchen whitened around her,
Like a cube of scrubbed sunlight,
White wood and red tiles.

In the end, it was ripe with silence,
This room stilled to a glow,
Smelling like an October morning
Wild with blackberries and streams.

THE KITCHEN (For My Grandmother) / by WILLIAM BEDFORD

When I was young the world was a little pond
Grandmother and red roof, the lowing
Of oxen and a bush made up of trees.
And all around was the great green meadow.

Lovely it was, this dreaming-into-the-distance,
This being nothing at all but air and wind
And bird-call and fairy tale book.
Far off the fabulous iron serpent whistled.

Translated from the German by Michael Hamburger

RETURN OF THE VILLAGE LAD / by ALFRED LICHTENSTEIN

Oma was sixty-three when I was born —
No one who knew
Eugenia Herrman Holm, neither child, grandchild, neighbor
Nor acquaintance could find a flaw. Her finely creased face,
Her cheek, the softest and most mystifying I ever kissed,
Her slow, soothing, cracked-mellow voice all invested me
With a deep wonder and deeper calm.
The house reflected her. Serenity, people said, such serenity
In that house. She was the gentlest woman I ever knew,
And those who had known her fifty years or more, they said so too.

from AFTERNOON IN WATERLOO PARK / by GERALD DUMAS

My mother's mother died
in the spring of her days. And her daughter
did not remember her face. Her portrait
engraved in my grandfather's heart
was struck from the world of images
after his death.

Only her mirror remains, sunk deeper with age
into its silver frame.
And I, her pale granddaughter, who do not resemble her,
peer into it today as if it were a pool
hiding its treasures
under the water.

Deep deep beyond my face
I see a young woman
pink-cheeked and smiling,
a wig on her head.
She is putting
a long earring into the lobe of her ear. Threading it
through a tiny hole in the delicate flesh.

Deep deep beyond my face
shines her eyes' bright gold.
The mirror carries on
the family tradition:
that she was beautiful.

Translated from the Hebrew by Robert Friend

FROM MY MOTHER'S HOUSE / by LEAH GOLDBERG

CONTENTS

808.81
G

Grandparents'
houses

$12.50

2 2 APR

808.81
G

Grandparents'
houses

$12.50

DATE	BORROWER'S NAME	
4 / 15/05	gradai	2 2 APR 2005
4/09	Sampson	

© THE BAKER & TAYLOR CO.